P9-CSH-347

MY HAPPY BIRTHDAY BOOK

LISA JAHN-CLOUGH

1 9 9 6

Houghton Mifflin Company Boston

For information about this and other Houghton Mifflin trade and
reference books and multimedia products, visit The Bookstore at
Houghton Mifflin on the World Wide Web at
(http://www.hmco.com/trade/).

            Library of Congress Cataloging-in-Publication Data

Jahn-Clough, Lisa.
  My happy birthday book / Lisa Jahn-Clough.

     p.   cm.

  Summary: A little girl celebrates her birthday with great
exuberance, describing everything she loves about this special day.
  ISBN 0-395-77260-5 (hardcover)
  [1. Birthdays—Fiction.]   I. Title.
PZ7.J153536My 1996
[E]—dc20   95-37602
          CIP
          AC

Printed in Singapore
TWP 10 9 8 7 6 5 4 3 2 1
Walter Lorraine *wℓ* Books

with thanks to my Mother

Today is a super-duper special day.

It's not Christmas.
It's not Valentine's Day.

There is no other day
like today.

Everyone smiles
and gives me presents.

I like presents.

I put on my crown.

I dance my happy dance.

I blow bubbles.

I toot my horn and make lots of noise.

I lead the parade.

The yummy cake awaits.

I make a wish and
blow out all the candles.

Today is my birthday!

YAY!!!

I sing, Tra-la-la-la!
Happy, happy, happy
Birthday to...

ME!

Me, me, me, me, me!